My New

# AL YANKOVIC
# Teacher and Me!

Illustrations by
## WES HARGIS

HARPER
*An Imprint of HarperCollinsPublishers*

The first day of school—it was finally here!
I wondered who'd be my new teacher this year. . . .

QUIET PLEASE

Then at 8:30 sharp, a tall stranger walked in.
He stood by the chalkboard and stroked his long chin.

$\pi = 3.141592653589793238462643383279502884197169399375105820974944$

Mr. Booth

CLASS
RULES

RULES
CONT'D

RULE 216
NO GUM
2 DEMERITS

He said, "I'm Mr. Booth, and I'm happy to say,
I'll be teaching you all about *fractions* today!
Now open your textbooks to page number three—"

And that's when he stopped, and he stared right at *me*!
He said, "You! Young man! Why's that filth on your shirt?
You can't come in my classroom all covered with dirt!"

I said, "Hi! Nice to meet you, sir! Billy's the name.
See, a funny thing happened before the bus came.

I was digging to China out in my backyard,

And I almost was there when—I hit something hard!

Well, I dug, and I dug, and I dug a bit more

And discovered the skull of a *real dinosaur*!

And I would've cleaned up, sir, but hey, I'm no fool—
I just *couldn't* be late on the first day of school!"

For a second or two Mr. Booth kinda froze.
Then he walked up to me, and he looked down his nose.
"I don't tolerate nonsense—no, not one degree—
And your story sounds *highly unlikely* to me."

PERIODIC TABLE

"Why, of *course* it's unlikely!" I said. "Oh, by far!
The awesome-est things in the world often *are*!

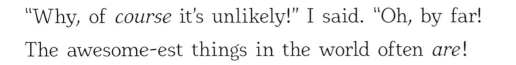

For instance, this friend of my third cousin Ned's
Got a farm where the dairy cows each have two heads!

That's so 'highly unlikely' the tourists all stop
Just to take their own pictures, at three bucks a pop!"

"Completely ridiculous!" sneered Mr. Booth.
"Please stop wasting our time and just stick to the truth!"

"Well, the truth *can* seem crazy—like that day in June
When my grandfather famously walked on the moon,

And he played ukulele while flying a kite:
It was in all the papers—you've heard of it, right?

You know what? My grandfather even implied
Someday he might take *me* along for the ride!"

The class started cheering, "Take *us*! Take us *too*!"
Then Mr. Booth bristled and snapped, "That'll do!
Pure poppycock! Class, please be quiet! Be still!
He is *not* going off to the moon—never will!"

"That's all right," I told him. "The moon is *okay* . . .
But I've been to a *much* cooler place anyway!

I just went on vacation with my dad and mom
To an island somewhere between Norway and Guam

Where the blueberry muffins grow right on the trees,
And you flip inside out every time that you sneeze.
All the rabbits say *moo,* and the poodles go *neigh,*
And the traffic-light colors are pink, blue, and gray.

Oh, and every third Thursday about half past one

All the gravity stops—wow, is that ever fun!

SQUIDTACULAR!!

There's a squid-eating contest—and hey, if you win it,

They let you be king for exactly one minute!

Then everyone does what you tell them to do

Man, I sure hope we get to go back next year too!"

Mr. Booth didn't care for that story one bit.
He furrowed his brow and said, "Okay, that's it!
Admit that your stories are simply absurd!
I just *do not believe* them—not *one single word*!"

Then I cleared my throat and said, "Well, sir, you know . . .
Just 'cause *you* don't believe doesn't mean it's not so!
Just 'cause you can't imagine it, that doesn't mean
That it simply can't be, or won't ever be seen.

I'll bet every great thinker and leader we've got
Could see *all* kinds of things other people could not!
So then why get upset if somebody like me
Tries to look at the world just a bit *differently?*"

"Enough!" Mr. Booth said. "No more of these stunts! You'll march *straight* to the principal's office at once!"

Something slipped from my book as I walked to the door.

Mr. Booth picked it up—

. . . and his jaw hit the floor!

It was me and a cow with not *one* head but *two*!
"Oh!" I said. "I was planning to give that to you!
It's a little good-luck gift—I got it for free!"

For my New Teacher
—Billy

He stared hard at the photo, then looked back at me . . .

For My New Teacher
-Billy

CLASS
RULES

QUIET

I avoided the principal's office that day.
In fact, ol' Mr. Booth put my gift on display!
He steals a quick glance at it once in a while,
And I'm not even kidding—I once saw him *smile*!

SLOW

We should get along fine, and it's certainly clear
There's a *lot* we'll be teaching each other this year—
Like how all of my stories are perfectly true!

. . . Except for, well, maybe a *detail* or two.